Still Maurey's Way

Monique. P

Still Maurey's Way

CASHKAKES PUBLISHING

Still Maurey's Way

ISBN- 978-1-7321382-2-3

Artist / Illustration: Kinia Homentowska

Creative Director: Tashuna Forbes

Message to Reader

To all of you who have read Maurey's Way Part 1, welcome back! To those of you who are new to the Maurey Series, Welcome and you might want to get caught up with Part 1 first but either way I know you will enjoy. This book will introduce you to several characters and unlike most stories, I want you all to feel like you are having a conversation with each character as they take you on their own individual journeys. Each Character has a story to tell and a point to prove and they want you to be the judge. As you get to know this bunch, I want you to enjoy and hold on to your seats because it will be a bumpy ride. Maurey is back and it's still her way! Enjoy and THANK YOU!

Dedication

This book is dedicated to anyone with hope and a dream. There is nothing that you can not do. God has allowed me to publish my 2nd book and to be honest had you told me this two years ago, I would say you were crazy. Hope is what is in our hearts, a dream is what is in our minds, but none of it means a thing if you don't believe. I dedicate this book to your success and your dreams coming true. I hope to inspire anyone to chase after their dreams. My prayers are that you never think the obstacles in life are bigger than the GOD that loves you. Also to the men and women

in prison, know that they can hold your
body but never your mind. BE FREE

I love you all!

DON'T GIVE UP!!

Acknowledgements

I want to do this part a little different. As if I am winning a Grammy, 1st, I just want to thank God my helper, my defender and my everything, I have seen so many dark roads and to be able to write a book, own a business, be a great mom and just be at peace is a testament that there is a God.

To the love of my life, my son Cashmere, for showing me a love I never knew existed in human beings, for pushing me, motivating me and being the glue that holds me together.

To my mom Big Monique, who had a rough life but somehow still remains full of love, I never told her this but she is probably reading it now crying, but thank you for fighting for us, thank you for not forgetting about your kids, for regaining the trust back, for doing everything you should have done with the 2nd chance God gave you but more than anything thank you for telling me who God is, for introducing me to the only solution to all my problems. You showed me what it was to be a real mother, I am still learning from you every day.

To my siblings, all 8 of you, I love you with all my heart and no matter where life takes us, we will always have each other. We disagree and we argue but what will never change is the love we have inside our hearts for one another. Thank you all for being there for me in one way or another from the beginning until the end.

To my best friends who support me in everything I do, no matter what it is, when I am in need they are there, the 4 of us have such a unique bond and it's a "sister ship" that I will cherish forever.

To my son's dad, he is my best friend we struggled together, we splurged together, we laughed, we cried and most importantly we had us a dope kid... I thank God for you.

To my Dad and grandad who are gone but will never leave my heart, everything they taught me helped mold me into the woman and mother I am today.

To my family related by blood, love and God I love you all.

To Anyone I have ever hurt, I am sorry and anyone who has ever hurt me...

Thank you...

I forgive you.

Love Monique Mable Plummer

Table of Contents

Table of Contents 2

Last Time with Maurey's Way

Love on the beach....

I had been back to page one, in the relationship area I was back to being alone, but I think I needed that time because I had put all my time and energy I had to spare into my growing business and things were flourishing and I felt my break was coming soon. People were booking me every week for parties and I was making more money than I ever had. Everything was perfect except the love life. One day at church, Money and I were in service and listening to the word and somebody came and sat next to Money and I looked to see who it was, and it was Cory and I just started crying. I couldn't believe he had stepped foot in a church after years of not being in church. I know he had taken that step and did it because he loved me and my son and for that I loved him even more. After church, Cory took me and Money to eat and when we got to the restaurant, I realized how nice of a place it was. I was feeling underdressed, I look at Cory and I'm like "baby this place is too fancy for what we have on" he just smiled and said we looked perfect don't worry. So as we are walking into the restaurant Money grabs my hand and says, "mommy I love you "I smile at him so big and reply "I love you more baby boy." As we finally get to the inside, I look up to see the decor and hear "surprise!!" It was my whole family, friends and all my loved ones in the restaurant with smiles and cheers all for me and I had not been so confused in my life because it was not July 6th my birthday had been passed. So I look back to see Cory to see what he was thinking or what he would say, and he was on one knee waiting for me to turn around. The tears just flooded, I couldn't believe after years of heart ache and pain, I was finally getting a chance to feel love of my own. Cory looked me in my eyes and said " Maurey, I love you , I love your son Money, You're so beautiful to me and loving , the way you love me makes me want to know the God you know so that one day I can understand what it's like to be completely at peace. You have been my peace for the last 2 years and I have been the happiest I have ever been with you. I don't know what the future holds but it's my prayer that God will allow you to be my wife... Will you marry me Maurey?" I just shook my head yes and the whole restaurant went crazy yelling and screaming shouts of joy. I looked over at Money and he put the thumbs up and I felt so good then I looked over to Trav and Nancy and he winked his eye at me for reassurance that I'm doing the right thing.

During the wedding day we all stood on the beach and I looked and felt so beautiful and I couldn't believe I was getting married to the love of my life. You know how people say, "sex on a beach" well I wanted the wedding theme to be "love on a beach" and this was definitely love on a beach. I was a little nervous, but I had to fight my fears and take chance on love. I spent my whole life losing the men I loved.

At this moment what was so important to me, was making my dad and my grandpa proud. My grandpa died when I was in college, around a month before the semester ended, he had gotten sick. I left school upstate and came down to help take care of him. My whole family loved my grandpa but him and I shared a special connection, I was the first grandchild he saw born, I was his twin, I looked just like him and acted just like him. He was there as my father because my dad was gone, I could go to my grandpa and no matter the problem he solved it. I never went without because my grandpa spoiled me. When he died, I think something in me died too and I still cry when I start thinking about him. He always said "get married, Maurey and finish college, don't be no damn dummy" lol I would laugh because he was a southern man and if you know southern men most are sweet, but they are real they have no filter. I had finally done one of the things he wanted me to do, it may have not been in order, but I did it. Now my next chapter is going back to school. I snapped out of my daze because thinking about my dad and grandpa at this moment will make me ruin this makeup.

The officiant stopped talking and asked the silly question I hate the whole "does anyone object to this union, blah blah blah speak now or forever hold your peace" so I just stand there waiting for her to finish because I know no one would dear do that and she goes to finish and I hear "WAIT I OBJECT! DON'T DO IT MAUREY" I didn't even turn my head because I knew that voice and I knew all hell was about to break loose. Everyone gasped and whispered, and I could see them looking from him to me waiting... He continued as he walked his way towards me and pushed off security... "I love you and I'm sorry and I..." before he could finish, I took off running in the opposite direction and Cory was running towards Don. I guess Don was so into watching me that he didn't notice Cory until it was too late, he punched Don so hard Don stumbled but he didn't hit Cory back. He knew he was wrong, but he didn't care he had to find me, so he went after me. I sat in the bathroom crying until my makeup was ruined and I had never felt so confused in my life. I knew I loved Cory he was perfect to me, something was always missing but I ignored it because I he was right for me. Don had apologized to me a billion times but the look in his eyes let me know he was really, sorry and all the feelings I thought were gone came rushing back like a stupid fool. I had no idea what to do with these feelings because I knew one thing Cory didn't deserve this, and I would never hurt him, so I had to make a tough decision and face the music. I walked back to where the wedding was, and all my family and Cory's family were talking, and Cory was sitting down with his hands on his head looking like he had just lost his best friend. Well I hope he didn't lose me, I don't know did he? I touched his shoulder to get his attention and he looked up with a half-smile and said, "you still love him, don't you?" I looked away and thought about how I would answer this, turning back I gazed right in his eyes and told him the truth...

To be continue....

Save Her for Me

Ever Since this clown crashed my wedding things have been so crazy between Maurey and I. I mean I love her with all my heart, but I couldn't marry her after I saw that look in her eyes...That look that has been hunting my dreams every night since that day. A look of relief, even though she cried until she ran out of tears and strength trying to convince me, but in my heart I new it was only me because it couldn't be him. Second best has never been me, so I left and been ignoring all her calls. Hell, everyone's calls have been on call block. I hear my phone ringing now, damn who's calling me now.

 The last person I'd think would be calling, my damn absentee father, this must be an emergency, let me pick up. "Hello?" I said into the phone annoyed. "yea son, I'm sorry about the wedding" ... I tried to interrupt him because I had gotten a billion, "I'm sorry about the wedding" text from everybody I ever known. My dad had a way of shutting you up, so when he talked, you listened so he kept going. "Just hear me out, I know how it is to feel like you're not good enough, like you're in a competition in your own mind, that only you know about. I know you probably don't want to hear it but it's what made me leave your mother. I hated her for years because I felt like I was just her second choice even after she spent years trying to prove that even though I was her second choice, I was a better choice. I pushed her away and I also pushed you kids away. I won't tell you to marry Maurey, I am sure you have given her your complete ass to kiss, because you're my son. Hell, she might not want you, but you've built a relationship with her son, so don't push him away because you'll never regain that trust again. Trust me I know." I knew he was referring to our estranged relationship. It made me think about my buddy Money, I hadn't realized how I had ignored him too. He has a father, a damn good one but him and I were best friends, I love that kid like he's my own and I love Maurey. My dad has been wrong my whole life, but today he was right. This wasn't about Maurey, it really was about me and my insecurities. It's been a month and I was ready to come home and marry my girl, if she will still have me. Damn I pray to God that he just please saves her for me.

Through with Love

Hey y'all its me Maurey! Times have been extra hard on me emotionally and financially; the wedding we paid for was a disaster but really who can I blame? We were supposed to move into the new apartment, it was my surprise to my would-be new husband. He hasn't been responding to my calls, he never answered his door, and had changed his job site at the construction company he works with. I had been paying the rent for my apartment in the projects, I know I should, but I'll never let it go. I guess half of me still holds on to my past and really you never know. I pray I don't have to go back to the projects, but I will always have a place to call home for my son. Never again would I put him through being homeless if I could help it.

The new apartment was beautiful and furnished, I paid the first month rent, security and furnished it with my savings. I thought we would make a new start in our new home that had enough room for all of us. Being that Cory made more than me, I knew he would take over the rent but seeing as he has been ignoring my calls, I had to pay the bills this month for both apartments, on top of all my bills, and my growing spoiled son Money. My poor baby boy, he doesn't understand all of this. It's been a month and I was done with Cory, I give up on him and love. What really made me make this choice wasn't because I never loved him, it wasn't because I really didn't want to get married, and it damn sure wasn't because I really wanted to be with Don... NO it was because of my son! My Baby boy who I have purposely kept sheltered and never allowed any other man I've dated meet, I let Cory into his world. I let him get to know him and they became best friends, they were close and had their own relationship outside of me. At least that's what I thought, to me he had to be just pretending just to be on my good side. I mean hell it worked, I was going to marry this man. Now, I would never take him back for the pain he caused my son by ignoring his calls, text messages, video calls and he even mailed him a letter to his apartment. He didn't hurt me as much as he hurt my baby, and nobody gets to do that, NOBODY! I was so done with his bitch ass, there was nothing him or anyone could even do or say. When I said something, trust it was final. What y'all thought? It's still Maurey's Way!

Mask Off

What's up, it's me Trav, I know y'all
heard what happened but damn I felt
bad for my baby mama. She had always
been the girl who worked so hard to
make people happy, she always gave
out good energy and vibes no matter
what she had going on. I felt like damn
if I hadn't fucked up all them years ago,
I would be the one she was in love with
and I could have protected her from all
of this.

Don't get me wrong, I love my wife but Maurey was my number one. You know I saw a movie and a man said, "you never get over the greats." Maurey was and will always be one of the greats, and nothing will ever change the love and respect I have for her. I did her so wrong, but we were kids, she forgave me, but I never forgave myself. I always felt like her life had been up and down, and it was all my fault. She is my best friend so really, I can't help but want to save her. Knowing Maurey, she is always going to have her way.

"Hey baby! What you over here thinking about?" Nancy said in her sweet voice. Which means she is horny, my wife was addicted to sex, so I know y'all going to think I'm crazy for answering her truthfully, when I said to her "Maurey". Her face said it all, but she tried to cover it up with her words, "aww baby I know, I feel so sorry for her." She continued... "It's like how such a good woman can have such bad luck with men?" I felt offended by her comment, not for me but for Maurey.

"Nah she doesn't have bad luck, the men that fuck up their chance with her do." I walked out the room to let her sit and think about what I just said.

I regret everyday how I did Maurey, she has been my best friend when I didn't even deserve her friendship so I will never let somebody play her, wife or not. See I wasn't going to marry Nancy but when I told Maurey I was thinking of proposing in hopes that she would finally let me back in, and let her guard down, she didn't. I don't know I guess part of me wanted her to tell me she didn't want me to do it, hell any sign, but all she did was the opposite and help me pick out the ring. That was Maurey though, anything she could do to help and ensure I was happy she would always do. Honestly to me it was my confirmation she didn't love me anymore, at least like how I had loved her. I'm no bitch or nothing but I teared up that night she helped me pick out the ring because I realized I had to let her go, and I did.

Fast forward, I marry the girl I thought was so sweet, so pure in heart, she was so understanding and not like other women when it came to my relationship with Maurey. At least that was what I thought, she doesn't know I over heard her laughing at Maurey with her ghetto ass friends. That shit damn near broke my heart to know I had married a fake ass chick. I mean I wish y'all would have heard her she was like "yea girl that bitch looked so stupid, what a hoe! How she had another nigga crash her wedding! Yes and her man is not speaking to her! GIRL YES, Trav stupid ass all over here calling her everyday sounding stupid. He all like Hey Maur, you ok? Hey Maur, y'all need anything? Sounding like a bitch! Girl yes! I am mad, I thought finally she could keep a man and leave mine alone..." I mean she went on and on and on with that annoying ass voice. Now my dick wouldn't even get hard for her.

Maurey doesn't know but I'm planning on divorcing Nancy. I have love for her but every time I hear her voice, I get annoyed. All that extra sweet shit was all a fake and if you can be that evil and fake a friendship, you can fake a marriage. Crazy part is, I never trusted her with My son Money, for whatever reason. I never felt like she was stupid enough to do anything to my baby boy, but I just felt like he didn't really take to her like that, so I didn't want to force it. Maurey would call that "God's spirit of discernment."

Crazy thing is, Maurey was the only one there for me and Nancy when she had lost baby number four. Four damn miscarriages, it never made sense but now I see God was giving me a sign all along. I must plan a dinner with my family, my baby boy Money and best friend Maurey and catch up. I know Maurey will know exactly what to say because I need her voice of reasoning. In the mean time I will start packing because trust me, shit about to hit the fan once I serve Nancy with these divorce papers. I might not be able to have Maurey but I'm not going to be miserable with a chick I can't trust. I know you are probably thinking I should just talk it out with her but what everybody don't know is you only have one chance to cross me and it's over. I always thought Nancy was so beautiful but damn who would have thought.

She took the Mask off ...

By Any Means

Damn I can't believe I crashed her wedding. I already know nobody is fucking with me after this, but I still want to tell my side. See Maurey and I have history and yeah, a nigga fucked up every time he got a chance, but I always expected her to wait for me.

Ever since I met her, I been in love with her but I'm an insecure nigga and never been afraid to tell her that. I don't trust nobody, shit I don't even trust my damn self.

So, every time I got around her, I had a feeling I never felt with another girl and that shit scared me because I knew she had the power to hurt a nigga bad if she ever wanted to. I remember getting mad when I heard she was fucking with somebody when we were younger, and we weren't even together. I told her ass lose my number and this bitch told me it was never even stored. No lie that shit killed me, I don't mean to call her a bitch, but she was a bitch at that moment. She thought I was mad because one of these bitches she used to chill with told me she said my dick was wack, but I knew if she said it, it was because she didn't want nobody to fuck with me. My dog ass ended up letting the same bitch hook me up with her friend and I knew that was gone piss Maurey off but as always, she was never phased.

It always felt like she had no emotions, like she is always good no matter what. She was always too cool and stand offish, nothing could hurt her. I know it probably sound like I was trying to hurt her, but I wasn't, and I would never do anything to just hurt her, but I wanted her to show me her emotions, get mad, curse me out, pop up at my house or something. Maurey would never allow me to see her hurt and that was why I couldn't trust her because she didn't trust me with her true feelings. No lie I stopped speaking to her for damn near a year, but I never could stop thinking about her. When we started speaking again, I would pop up every few months just to see if I still had her and I did.

I just always felt like she was mine, but I was moving real fucked up back then. I was paying her ass no mind half the time just because I guess it made me feel better knowing she wanted me and was willing to do whatever to be with me. Like I said I was insecure, that shit catered to my ego a bit, but after a while when I stopped calling, she never reached out like she usually did. No holidays, no birthdays, nothing she just went ghost.

Last month I was feeling like shit after I saw her best friend and she told me

Maurey was getting married. I had called Maurey and her number kept going to voicemail and now I realized she had fucking blocked me. I tried to hit her on every social media account she had, and the messages was never answered. Damn I realized I love her, and she is the one for me. I fucked it up chasing money and bitches and searching for what I already had. Maurey was the only one who always saw the good in me and knowing she didn't look at me the same was killing me.

I have to do something before it's too late. My home girl is married to her baby father and she told me Maurey is still single and that stupid nigga didn't take her back. I felt bad knowing it was my fault, but I feel like I exposed that man's weakness because he left her at the wedding after they made me leave and he hasn't spoken to her since. To be real I didn't care, that's his problem because now that he was out the way I had to earn Maurey's love and trust back. My homegirl Nancy, Trav's wife is cool, and y'all know Trav is Maurey's baby father but they are all cool like a blended family, so I trust her. Well she was giving me some advice and ideas on how to get Maurey back and I am considering them. Let me call her because she said she would help me with the plan and make sure I get my girl back. I hope this shit work because I need Maurey back in my life.

By Any Means!

Little Secrets

Hey guys it's me Tasha, remember me?
I am Maurey's best friend. I can't
believe my friend's wedding got
crashed. You wouldn't even believe me
when I say I feel like crap. The reason
that is, is because I was the one who
told Don about the wedding. I know you
all are thinking the same thing I am
feeling and to answer the obvious
question, I don't know why I opened my
big ass mouth. I had no idea he would

be bold enough to do some shit like that. I feel like an idiot. I really should have kept my mouth shut and now I can't even look my friend in her eyes. I have to tell her the truth because it is killing me, I hope she will forgive me, because you all know how she is, it's like cross her once and she never looks at you the same. Let me at least tell my side and you guys be the judge.

What happened was I ran into Don at the mall and was trying to make him feel like the piece of shit he is. So I was out shopping for the last-minute things

I needed for the wedding and he had stopped me talking about how he has been calling Maurey and she wasn't answering and blah blah blah. I was acting all oblivious and shit until I saw a chick that we know from the block stop and talk to him. She rolled her eyes at me and was being real, extra. I shook my head and decided to burst both of their damn bubble. I kindly said, "well Don let me go, I have to get the rest of the things I need for Maurey's wedding, when I speak to her, I'll let her know you were looking for her." I walked off enjoying the dumb ass looks on both of their faces, that bitch was so mad he was asking for my girl Maurey, and him oh my goodness he looked like he had shitted on himself. Now that I think about it, I should have known by that crazy ass look in his eyes that he was gone find out where Maurey's wedding was at and ruin it.

I just don't understand how he found out where it was because Maurey didn't invite everyone, she wanted it to be intimate, so the location was supposed to be a secret. Now all I can do is stress about this and can't even tell my friends about what is going on with me.

I am engaged to the love of my life Greg and I can't even enjoy it. My guilt won't let me because I feel like if it wasn't for me, Maurey would be enjoying the life of a newlywed. Greg is beefing with me because I haven't been wearing my engagement ring and he is pissed that I haven't told my girls yet. He thinks I don't want to marry him but that is crazy because I literally adore him and damn near worships the ground he walks on. I have to cook for him tonight and tell him what is going on so he can understand and hopefully give me some time to get the truth out to Maurey. The thing is I am afraid to tell Greg, because Greg is Cory's best friend, so you see why I haven't told him yet. I don't want him to be mad at me because he always goes crazy when it comes to Cory. Cory's family took Greg in when his mom was using drugs, so he sees Cory as his brother, and he feels like he owes him, so he sometimes is very over protective.

I feel like Greg will blame me just like Maurey and don't get me wrong because I blame myself, but I don't know I guess I feel like maybe it happened for a reason. Cory has trust issues and it shouldn't have been that easy to leave Maurey. Maurey also has to let go of that jack ass Don completely. However, If Maurey or Greg heard me say that, they would really kill me so I will just keep that to myself. Either way I have to figure out a way to break the news to both Greg and Maurey without them both hating me and figure out a way to announce my engagement so that way my crazy ass fiancé will get off my back about wearing this ring. You all wish me luck because I just have a bad feeling about this. I miss my mom; may she rest in peace. She was wise and would know what to say. I can hear her voice in my head, "little secrets start big trouble" I have to come clean...

Pray for me

Strength or Weakness

This shit is all fucked up, damn I can't believe what happened to Maurey. I am pissed with Don's stupid ass! Oh trust me it is on sight when I see him. I may be small in size, but people know how I give it up, my hands are deadly. Oh yeah, how rude of me, let me introduce myself. Hey guys I am Kim, Maurey's cousin and best friend. I am like the glue that holds me and the girls together. Everyone says I am the voice of reasoning, I actually hate that, but I guess I am glad that I have the ability to keep things in perspective for those I love.

To be honest though sometimes I feel like if I am always strong for everyone, who the hell is going to be strong for me? I can't be weak around my girls or family, they need me to be the strong one, so for them, that is what I am. However, right now I am not as strong as I seem to be, I am going through a lot that I don't want to tell my family or friends about. My health has always been good but last month I felt a lump in my breast, and it was right around the time of Maurey's wedding so I knew I couldn't tell anyone. They did run a test and I am on my way now to get the results. Being alone in this situation is killing me but I can't deal with my friends or family right now. They will be all dramatic and will try to make me feel like I am this needy, sick person and I hate that vulnerable feeling. I've been through so much and half of the people that are closest to me would never know. I don't mean to be so closed in but like I said, I just hate people feeling sorry for me, and I hate vulnerability.

My state of mind is always strong, and I am always feeling like no matter what it is, I will be ok but today I will tell you, I am scared, and I feel bad within even admitting that. Well let me go in this doctor's office and hear the results. Whatever it is, I know God will see me through. "Hello, Ms. Kim, can I call you Kim?" the doctor asked as I had my head down saying a prayer. I looked up and for the first time in my life I felt speechless. I mean yes right now is not the time to be thinking about a man but damn if he didn't look good, this doctor was some out of the movies fine, he looked like Trey songs a little bit and I could barely respond but I found my voice and told him yeah, he can call me Kim. What I was really thinking was you can call me whatever you want at this point looking like that. Child talk about bad timing, I was in the doctor's office about to hear my fate staring at him like he was my date. Doctor Fine led me into the room and told me to have a seat. I snapped out of my trance and got serious. "Ok Ms. Kim, My name is Dr. Jay it's short for Jaron whichever you'd prefer. I was looking at the scans and test results and I just wanted to discuss everything with you. So unfortunately we did find cancerous cells and we do need to operate fast to remove it before it spreads." Dr. Jay was talking but all I saw was his lips moving and next thing I know everything went black.

Apparently, I had passed out and when I came to, I looked up to see Dr. Jay's beautiful face but the look on it was so annoying. He felt sorry for me and I hated when people felt sorry for me. I jumped up and saw that I had all these wires and iv on me and was scared and confused. Dr. Jay must have read my mind, because he came to my side and put his hand on my back to console me and let me know it was just fluids because I was dehydrated, and the wires were monitoring my pressure. At this point I was replaying what I last heard him tell me, over and over again, like really? me with cancer? How could this happen to me? I was the person everyone thought was perfect and I'm sick with this ugly disease. Dr. Jay interrupted my thoughts, "Ms. Kim, do you have anyone to call? Maybe your husband or boyfriend?" now any other time I would be happy to have him fishing to see if I was single but knowing what I know, I was out of it. I just shook my head no to answer him. I looked him in his eyes and let him know, I had nobody to call and just couldn't hold back my tears. To feel like this with all the people in my life, was heartbreaking. I was alone in my mind because I couldn't add this on anyone's plate right now.

Dr. Jay told me If I wanted to get a second opinion I could but if not, I needed to schedule the surgery right away. I just told him to schedule it because the sooner the better. I was so zoned out I didn't hear him asking me if I needed a ride. I finally snapped out of planning my funeral and realized he was staring at me. "Ms. Kim are you okay to go home? I can drive you, because I am getting off early to pick up my daughter." I dropped my head and nodded yes, partially because I did need a ride and hated that I needed him but also disappointed that he had a kid and probably a wife. Looking like that I should have known this man was taken.

On the way home Dr. Jay was quiet, he didn't say much until I turned to him and was about to thank him and before I could he started talking. "You are a beautiful, strong woman and I can tell that you are strong because you have had over a dozen missed calls after you passed out, so I know you have people who love you, but you came by yourself. Sometimes being too strong can be your weakness. My wife told me that before she died. She had refused all cancer treatment and wanted to fight it naturally because she felt like the Chemo and surgery would make her too weak and she wanted to be able to function for our daughter. It killed her and losing her killed me inside and left me a single dad. For years I was too prideful to ask for help but eventually I realized I couldn't do it on my own and finally let my mom and sisters help me with my daughter Kayla. I am telling you this because I know you don't want to ask for help but you don't want to go through this alone, here is my card with my personal number if you ever need to talk and remember you come back in two weeks for the surgery and you will need somebody with you." Dr. Jay had said a mouth full and pulled up right by my building just in time because I was speechless. I had never had a man read me like that and I definitely never met one that could make me feel like this in less than 24hrs of knowing him. I took his card and went to shake his hand, but he pulled me in for a hug and I just melted. I mean even in this moment knowing my life just changed for the worse, I felt warm and safe in his embrace. I finally let go and just smiled and left. What a day, I have to tell my girls, and my family but not today. Right now I just need to take it all in and have a still moment to talk to GOD.

A Woman Scorn

The Nerve of this man to serve me with
divorce papers, at my job and move out
without even telling me why. I know
this has something to do with that Bitch
Baby mother of his, Maurey. Oh by the
way if you haven't guessed already, I
am Trav's wife Nancy, I don't really care
what anyone thinks of me because I
wasn't always like this. He made me

this way and now he thinks he can leave me and run off in the sunset with her? Ever since I met him, I have been in Maurey's shadow, he always compares us and always wants me to be more like her. I was shocked she was ok with the whole blended family idea I had, but truthfully it was because I like to keep my enemies close. Now fast forward years later, and after all I have done to be with this man, BOOM! he just leaves me with no explanation.

I have been calling Trav and anybody who knows him nonstop. I haven't gotten anyone to answer me but surprisingly, Maurey did. She is acting all clueless, pretending to feel sorry for me and all that phony shit she loves to pull. I'm letting her think she is playing me but Little do she know she is about to disappear for a little while so I can get my man back. My ex boo Max from high school is a real hood street nigga and he is the one I was telling Don I can hire to kidnap Maurey. Oh wait did I forget to mention that I told Don he is an actor but really, and truthfully, he is my crazy little pet that sweats me and will do anything just to even smell this coochie. I told Max that if he kidnaps Maurey for me and keeps her away that eventually I will leave Trav for his money and we will be together. Really, what is going to happen is, I am going to let Max take the fall for the kidnapping and he will go away for a long time or Don will kill him. I don't care either way because While Maurey is away, Trav will be so out of it he will come right back to me, I will console him in his time of need, and we will be a big happy family again. Maurey will be found once I make an anonymous call telling the cops and Don's sick puppy love ass where to find her, he will look like he is saving her, and she will be his problem. Just in case the plan doesn't go my way I told Max to drug Maurey, she has never done drugs ever so I know there's a chance she will get hooked. If she does, I know Trav will never want her and really, I doubt any man will. Trav will have to take his son little Money and I can show him that I can be a good mother.

One way or another I am going to get my man back. All the miscarriages I done had really has made me feel less than a woman and he doesn't make it any better parading his baby mother and their son around me all the time. It has hurt me, and I have become somebody I thought I would never be but it's too late, I can't lose Trav and I don't care what it takes. The kidnapping is happening tomorrow and there is nothing anyone can do to stop it.

Girl Fight

Today all the girls decided to take me out to make me feel better about the wedding and just all that has been going on but really as I look in the eyes of my friends, my sisters, my ace boon coons. I can tell they are all hiding something or going through something and don't want to add stress to me, so they are hiding it. I am the friend that can read anyone. Kim thinks she is so secretive, and nobody knows but I just don't pressure her to talk because I feel like when she is ready, she will. Tasha is up under me like all of the time, but she has something to tell me because she can't give me eye contact and I don't know why but I always know when Tasha is guilty, she will start to act so obvious about it. Now Sam is a whole different vibe. She is my newest best friend that we all voted in to our group years ago. Sam is the turn up girl, so I understand her acting different because she just had a baby. Sam has been so busy with her new bundle of joy that I can tell the only thing going on with her is that she needs some sleep. I have to talk to all of them and today they will be forced to spill the beans. Everybody is catering to me and I'm sick of it, its been over a month and honestly, I am ok. Everything happens for a reason so what can I really do? I know I won't spend another day with my family and friends tip toeing around me afraid to even mention Cory or the word wedding around me.

So we all sit at the table and Sam is just looking out of it, so I start with her. "Ok so I have to talk to you all and I don't want any interruptions so please let me just get it all out. Sam! I feel some type of way, you just had my little niece and have been keeping her away from me, you made all of us the God mother and I have yet to watch Baby Kacey for you. Now you always look tired, your man is working extra hard with his cleaning business and instead of you calling me to help, you have been struggling with the kids on your own. Now it stops today, I am off on Sundays and will be getting my God child to give you a break for a few hours.

Now Kim, you are the strongest woman I know and after a life time of friendship you still don't trust us to tell us much about you. We all respect the way you are because we know you hate us feeling sorry for you but as your friend, your sister, my damn cousin I'm demanding you right now to tell us what's been going on with you. You look like you have been stressing out and that is never you, let us be there for you how you are always here for us.

Now, Tasha, Tasha, Tasha. I simply have one question. What did you do and why are you afraid to tell me? I have known you girl since we were in the park playing freeze tag and the same way you couldn't look us in the eye when you tried to pretend you weren't "it" is the same way you can't look me in my eyes now. Now I love you all and I need us all to be united right now in our lives and support each other."

I took a deep breath and looked at all of them letting them know I was done. I had said a mouth full, so now it was their turn to start talking because they know I wasn't trying to hear anything else but the truth. Sam went first, telling us how she thinks she is going through postpartum and she is afraid to tell her man Jason, or anyone because she feels like a bad mother. She stays up all night with the baby and can't sleep because she feels so guilty about the feelings she is having. She thinks that she is going crazy, but we all assured her that she is not and right at that moment We made an appointment with the doctor who helped Tasha when she was going through it after our niece was born. Now we all hugged her and promised we will be coming around more often, to check on her and the kids.

Next was Tasha, she kept avoiding eye contact and finally the water works came. I mean you would have thought we was at a funeral the way sis was crying. We all know how she is so we let her cry because trying to console her will only make her cry longer. She finally stopped and we were all worried because it had to be bad. She looked at me and just confessed her soul. She told me how she ran into Don and was stunting on him and his chick and let him know I was getting married, how she felt it was all of her fault and she has been over obsessing about it for weeks, how she got engaged and won't wear her ring. She started telling us how Greg is mad at her and hasn't been speaking to her because he said she has a big mouth and its her fault his best friend is going through this. She was saying sorry a million times, telling me she promised she didn't tell Don, the address and she doesn't know how he found out and she can't celebrate her own engagement knowing that she ruined my life. That was all I got out of the crying and crying and more crying. I mean to be honest me a month ago would have beat Tasha ass because I needed somebody to blame, me a month ago would have gassed myself into thinking if it wasn't for her, Cory and I would be living happily ever after. The reality is, Cory wasn't ready for a forever because if he was it wouldn't have ever been that easy for him to leave me like that and never look back for me or my son.

I was madder that my best friend hid her engagement, that the moment of joy and celebration had been stolen from her. I'm mad I couldn't have had this conversation sooner, so she didn't have to beat her self up so bad. After she was done, she looks around, down then finally at my face, I had to fuck with her, so I had the stink angry face on. She was so sad I couldn't help it, I bust out laughing. "Bitch you getting married!! Pull that fucking rock out and let me see it!" I told her. She smiled so bright and the other girls laughed, and we oohed and awed at her ring and I just let her know I love and forgive her and its not her fault. I gave her some advice on how to deal with Greg, we have to pay the lingerie section a visit after this.

Now Kim was all pretending to be soooo into everybody else drama so she can avoid speaking on her own. She knows me better than that, so I brought the attention right back to her and she just sat there I guess trying too figure out how to tell us whatever it was she was hiding. After what felt like forever, I saw the tears falling from her eyes and we all looked at each other in total shock. Now please understand Kim is my strongest friend, she always knows the right thing to say and do. I have never seen her show any emotion like this before other than angry when a chick acts up and she has to show them she is crazy with the hands. We all got up to console her and she put her hand up to stop us. We were so confused because we wanted to respect her wishes but we wanted to be there for her.

I am just always the one who does what I want, I mean duh this is Maurey's way, so I pushed her hands down and hugged her. I mean I thought she might have wanted to swing on me, but she just cried and cried in my arms and the girls came around and joined the hug. She finally stopped and calmed herself down to tell us that the doctors told her she had cancerous cells in her breast, and they need to remove the lump because it may spread. Nothing made sense, she was the healthiest person I knew, always ate good and kept her body fit, how could she be sick? She told us she met a man and fell in love, he just so happened to be her doctor, but she is afraid to even tell him how she feels. This was starting to be a lot for all of us, here we are best friends all going through hell by ourselves when we could have helped each other get through together.

I was once again kicking my ass for not having this conversation sooner. After hearing everything Kim had to say we all cleared our schedule. Sam called her mom and begged her to watch the kids, Tasha told Greg to get their daughter and hold her down, I called Trav and he got little Money for me and we all went home to pack a small bag for a much-needed girls' sleepover. We needed to be with each other for at least 24hrs and just gather all of this and figure out how we are going to fight back and regain our lives and peace.

On my way home I called Nancy to cancel our lunch because my girls needed me. I felt bad because I really know she needed somebody, I had told her I didn't know where Trav was but really, he was at my old apartment. He took over the rent and have been staying there. He won't tell me why he is leaving Nancy, he said he would tonight over dinner but that has to wait. Nancy left me a voicemail crying telling me how she wants to kill herself and I decided to just go to their house to talk her through this. I know she is my ex's wife, but she is family and just a lost soul.

Trav told me her mom was never really there for her emotionally, she just wanted to be her friend instead of a parent, her dad was a dead beat and she is always falling out with her friends. I know she needed me, so I texted my ladies and told them to meet me at Kim's while I run to Nancy and make sure she is ok.

Ride or Die

I was going in Nancy and Trav's building and I had the weirdest feeling like somebody was watching me. No lie I kept turning around and thought maybe I was being paranoid but for my own peace of mind I had the knife my brother Mitch gave me. He is crazy but he taught me to always go with my gut. I got to their floor and was so out of breath from the stairs, so I stopped and out of nowhere some motherfucker grabbed my ass in a headlock from the back. He was putting me to sleep and I knew by the way he was choking me up, I used the last of my energy to stab his ass in the side, I think it was his side. Then I was out. By the time I came to I was tied to a chair with my eyes covered and my mouth gagged. I just started praying and begging God to get me back to my son safe and if anything happened to me to just help my son be the man, I tried my best to raise him to be. After my prayers and some tears thinking about my son, I went into survival mode and had to think of a plan. I'm listening to the sounds, and I'm hearing a voice. It's a man and he must be on the phone because he is talking but I don't hear the other person responding. "This bitch Stabbed me Nan, I need a doctor I'm losing blood. You told me she was a church going bitch, she stabbed me with a fucking warrior knife. Nan, I love you but I'm not about to die in here over this bitch. Figure it out and call me back." He had kept calling the person Nan and all I could think about is how I was in Nancy's building and got kidnapped. This stupid bitch set me up! I figured that much out but for what? I mean it's not like it's my fault Trav left her. Trav... damn I hope him, and my son Money is ok. I hear footsteps nearing me, so I play like I'm still knocked out and hang my head.

SLAP!!!

I mean when I say this strong ass man just slap the life out of me with all his strength. I felt my head starting to hurt, and I had a feeling he was going to do more but I wouldn't cry, I been through too much shit to let this loser see me cry. I heard him laughing and it started to piss me off. Then like the true coward he started to try and break me down.

"Bitch by the time I'm done with you, nobody will want you. I heard you a drug free type of church bitch. Well you better say a prayer because things are about to get really interesting." He kept going and going about how once he gets me out the way he can finally be with his bitch Nan. He even said they are going to milk Trav for all of his money from his business in the divorce. Trav has this talent agency that he started two years ago that is doing really well, he has helped so many artists get signed, modeling contracts and acting gigs. At this point I realized what kind of fool I was dealing with. He wanted to make himself feel big and bad and he wanted to do that by breaking me down.

He's a little on the slow side though and has a big mouth because he had just told me their whole plan. He just keeps talking and talking and I think he was getting high because I smelled weed but it had to be laced because it had a funny smell. I was feeling so sick to my stomach and getting nervous about what he was going to do to me. I Felt him coming closer, but I couldn't see because of the blindfold, I was trying my best to get my hands out of this rope. I finally loosened it, but I stayed put because his phone rung and he walked away. Normally I would have tried to fight but I was weak and tired. His phone ringing gave me enough time to take the blindfold off to see where I was. I was looking and it seemed like I was in some damn basement but where? I have to play my cards right and plan my escape because I will not be getting drugged or killed here. I spot my pocketbook but its too far for me to try to get my phone because this clown will see me. I put the blindfold back and put my hands back behind me and I'm listening to him talk to somebody but it's not Nancy because he is being real hostile. "Nigga what the fuck you mean where your girl at? I don't know what the fuck Nan told you but this damn sure isn't no game. This bitch about to get drugged and probably fucked because she is looking good. Man check this shit out, I don't give a fuck bout what you are saying, Nan said the bitch stays so she stays. "

I didn't understand what was going on, but I know that I don't have much time because this guy is crazy, and Nancy really has him under a spell because he hates me, and I don't even know him. What I do know is that I stabbed him, and he is losing blood, before he comes back let me look around for a weapon. I spot a dam tool box, so I rush over quietly and grab a hammer and say a quick prayer.

I hear him walking back and just in time I get the blindfold back in place and I have my hands behind my back and I'm ready for war. I have to get back to my son by any means and I will not leave this earth without a fight.

He starts talking his shit and I hear him mention how my nigga so fucking stupid, and how he thinks that he gone play captain save a hoe and its starting to really throw me off. Somebody I know other than Nancy is setting me up. I have to get him to talk. I start him up the only way I know how.

I start making sounds through the gag to get his attention so he can take it off and he does. I start talking "Please sir, I don't know what I did to you or Nancy, but I am sorry, please I need to get home to my son. Whatever your boss and Nancy is paying you, I promise my son's father will pay double!" I already knew he was about to be mad I called the mystery person his boss and boy was he. "Bitch that nigga isn't my boss! That's your punk ass nigga who hired me to fake kidnap you but me and my Nan had better plans for you. Matter fact I already said too much but don't worry you won't remember after I give you this hit!" he finished that last statement with a chuckle and walked off.

I will die before I let this flunky drug me, my body can't handle drugs I can't even smoke Reggie weed, I have never popped pills or anything. When he comes my way its going to be a fight, I can tell he is losing strength in his voice because of the blood he is losing so I have an advantage. I hear him on the phone with Nancy telling her to hurry up and that he is about to drug me now. I am getting myself ready for the fight that I know will be for my life, he starts walking my way and I know he has the drug in his hand. I am getting prepared, he bends down in front of me and I can feel him staring me down and as soon as he goes to touch me, I take the hammer and swing it from behind my back with full force.

WHACK!!!

I hear him fall and I jump up, take the blindfold fully off and the sight before me has me so sick to my stomach I throw up right beside his body. The hammer's pointy part is stuck in his head and blood is everywhere, I think he is dead. I see the crack needle or whatever he was trying to shoot up in me on the floor and I pick it up. I go to grab my purse and I am panicking trying to rush the fuck out of there when all of a sudden, I get attacked from the back of me. The person is smaller, but they are raining blows on my head with a damn gun, I think.

At this point I fell, and I am in the fetal position waiting for the blows to finish, with the crack needle still in my hand I am ready to strike. If this is my final blow before I die, at least know I fought until the end to get back to my son. Its Nancy because I hear her shoes walk around me and she bends down to see if I am dead or knocked out and as soon as she is close enough, I take the little strength in me and stab her ass with the crack needle right in her neck and pushed that shit.

Nancy has this crazy ass look on her face and her eyes roll behind her head and she falls out. I think she is about to overdose or something because her body is shaking, and she is foaming out of the mouth. I don't know why but I look around to find something to help Nancy, I feel sorry for her. I pick her up and run to the bathroom, throw her in and let the cold shower run on her hoping it will shock her, but I think it's too late. "Damn Nancy why did you do this! "I say out loud to nobody but myself.

Love and War

I don't know what to do but I call 911 and I hope they don't take me to jail for killing them. I hope they believe me that I was just defending myself. I grab my bag and call the last person I should have ever been calling, but the only person I know that will help me... Don.

As I am calling Don, I hear kicking and banging of the basement door and I hear the phone ringing and I realize its Don trying to get in. I start remembering what that crazy ass guy was saying to the person on the phone that was working with Nancy, and I start thinking about how the hell Don knew where to find me. This nigga is trying to kill me too? I go grab the gun that Nancy was hitting me with and I'm ready for War. I have the gun drawn and he finally kicks the door down and when he lays eyes on me, he has this look in his face, something I don't think I ever seen. He had love and fear in his eyes. I look at him and I don't know how to feel.

"WHY DON?" I ask him because I need to know. He doesn't respond looks around, sees the dead bodies and smiles. I shoot up to the ceiling to get his attention back to answering my question. He looks back to me with admiration almost and asks "Maurey, you did this?" I shake my head yes letting him know yes, I did kill two people in here. "Good girl..." he says, I look at him like he is crazy and repeat my question but this time I am screaming

"WHY DON?!!" he drops his head and starts telling me how Nancy had been cool with him since they were younger and she was the one who told him where the wedding was. Nancy had convinced Don to hire an actor to kidnap me, and for him to come save me and I would finally take him back. He kept saying sorry, he would never do anything to hurt me and how he didn't know Nancy hated me. Don had really made a deal with the devil and I don't understand why he thought saving me would make me take him back but if he ever had a chance in hell, he for sure lost it. Even though he didn't mean for this to happen he could have gotten me killed. I look at Don and I see the love that he never showed me before, the feelings that he always hid. He has never fought for me but today, and the day of my wedding proved to me that although he didn't have his shit together like Cory or Trav he was willing to do anything to be in my life and for that I will always love him. I looked him in the eyes and said "I forgive you Don, but we could never be together, I love you no matter what. You have to know that things have gone too far, and it just won't work, I need you to leave before the cops get here and I will never mention you had anything to do with this to a soul, I swear."

Just like that the love in his eyes had left and it was dark again. I didn't know what he was thinking, I never could figure him out so when he started walking towards me, I got scared and aimed the gun at him again. He hung his head in defeat and told me he loved me. He didn't want to go, but he knew I couldn't be with him, not after all he had done. He had pushed me away and ironically, he was the only man that had ever fought for me.

I had the gun still aimed because I just didn't know at this point what would happen next but as he was walking out the cops bust through the door. "Freeze!" one cop says, and Don tries to Come back towards me, and I am just still in shock. My mind is telling me to drop the gun, but I can't move, I am so scared. Another cop yells "she's got a gun!!" next thing I know I drop the gun and they shot me. Don tried to shield me, but it was too late, I was hit. All the moments in my life started to flash in my head like a slide show. I could hear Don yelling for me to fight and don't let go, I was slipping away. I knew it was my time because I was peaceful and no longer panicking, I was thinking about my son and how this will break his heart and that made me shed a tear and I could feel Don wipe it and then everything went black.

Darkness comes to light

Don

In my Mind I thought I was doing the right thing, I wanted to fight for Maurey and give her the love that she deserved. This bitch Nancy hated her the whole time and was using me to ruin her life and now it was all my fault. I was in handcuffs on my way to jail for trying to kill the cop that shot Maurey. Seconds before I was holding her begging her to fight and one tear rolled down her eyes and she was gone. I wiped the tear and shed a few of my own. My eyes zoomed in on the cop that killed my girl and lost it. I had revenge on my mind and nothing or nobody could stop me. I would have been successful, but I was out numbered.

They eventually whipped my ass and locked me up but the only pain I felt was in my heart. My life would never be the same, I lost the only woman who loved me for me. They were taking me out the house and I shed a few more tears for Maurey, as they were driving me to the bookings. I had no fear of what would be my fate, I just wanted to get her face out of my head, I only wanted to remember her smile and the love in her eyes when she saw me, not the look of fear she had when she pointed that gun at me when I tried to hug her. I closed my eyes and just started thinking about all of the good times we had and how I had spent most of the years running from real love because I was afraid. I am going to have to live with that for the rest of my life.

OFFICER DAVID

The crime scene looked so crazy. I was the officer who first arrived on the scene. I was looking at how beautiful this girl was, I couldn't believe my trigger-happy partner had killed this innocent kidnapped victim. He is going to be fried by the media for this, I always tell him to assess the scene before he starts shooting. Turns out she was kidnapped and set up and had gotten free to call the cops and had the gun up to protect her from her ex that she thought was there to hurt her.

The woman was a young mother, a business woman and connected to a few well-known people, the news is going to eat this story up. As I was collecting evidence and waiting for the slow ass coroner, I heard a moan and looked over to see that this woman was still alive. I call in for the medics, it had only been 5 minutes or so, but it felt like forever. The ambulance was still not here. Damn I hate the Bronx, I became a cop to protect the people in these areas and I always felt like they were so underserved. I made a call and decided I wasn't waiting on them because this girl has a chance. I picked her bloody body up and put her in my car and drove her my damn self. Rushing to the hospital it still seemed as if she was out of it but breathing. I rushed in the emergency entrance.

"HELP! HURRY!" I yelled and the doctors and nurses came and rushed her out of the car, and they went straight to the operating room.

I had blood all over me, so I went to go wash my hands and then instead of going back I decided to wait. They came in with the other woman they thought was dead, she had overdosed, and I guess everybody assumed she was dead, but she was in a coma. Both women were in a coma, the guy that we locked up had told us everything, so she was handcuffed to her bed. She was beautiful too, I don't see how somebody so beautiful could be so damn evil. Had to be something crazy that turned her that way.

I walked to the victim's room, I watched her connected to all of those machines, but she was fighting. I had a good feeling about her making it, she had survived her kidnapping even out numbered. I sat down and soon as I closed my eyes, I heard the door swing open and some man rushed in and he was crying and begging Maurey to wake up. He had a ring and put it on her finger telling her he was sorry and how he should have never left her at the altar.

 Next three women rushed in and they were all crying and crying begging her to wake up, talking to her. Her family came in and it was more tears and praying and begging for her to wake up. Lastly a man came in with a little boy. Somebody was trying to stop him from bringing the son in, but he gave them the look of death and they backed up. He asked us all to leave, I told him I was to be at her side at all times for her own protection and it was an order but really, I just wanted to be nosey. I heard him and their son say a prayer and he started to talk to her and confess his love for her and how he should have never done her wrong and marry another woman. He felt it was all his fault and he was begging her to please wake up for their son. It was the son's turn and even though he was young when he started to talk it was like he was a grown man.

Maurey

I was in a coma, all I saw was darkness. I knew that my family and friends were hurting. They were crying, praying and begging me to wake up and I was trying my best. It was nothing I could do. My baby boy started talking to me and I was so surprised by how big my boy Money had gotten. He started with a prayer and was saying it so fervently. He had me crying inside, I don't know if my body was making tears, but I knew my heart was crying because I wanted to wake up so bad for my baby.

To be honest I heard everybody that I loved begging me but hearing my son pray for me and talk to me like this let me know I'm not ready to die, I have to continue to raise him the way God wanted me to, I have to be here to witness the fruits of my labor. I was going to wake up I started begging God for help and right there in my own mind I promised I would continue to keep God first and raise my son to do the same, and I begged for forgiveness for killing Nancy and that guy, before I could finish my prayer I thought about the story of Job in the bible where Job had prayed for the friends who were treating him bad and that is how he was restored his health and everything the devil had took, God restored double.. it made me think about Don and Nancy, I loved both of them but for different reasons they had conspired against me, I know Don didn't know but he had really allowed Nancy to get in his head and ruin my life. Nancy was pretending the whole time because she loved Trav so much, but she was always in my shadow, I know she drove herself crazy thinking I was going to steal Trav from her and all the pain her mother put her through growing up, I'm not even mad at her, I feel bad for her.

I decided to do like Job and pray for them and beg God to forgive them for their sins and really, I wanted Don to be a free man, and Nancy to be free in spirit and go to heaven and not be punished for this eternally. I felt myself crying for Nancy and Don too lost souls and finished my prayer. "Amen" I said, but I heard it, then my son started yelling for his dad to go get the doctors because he heard me too. I was up! God had woken me up out of my coma and literally healed me just like Job. Oh I started thanking God in my head with great joy because I couldn't do much moving and talking, I just laid there with my eyes full of joyful tears.

The doctors rushed in and ran test, they made everyone leave except a cop. He was beautiful oh God forgive me damn near on my death bed I'm over here lusting over this man. I guess he was probably going to lock me up for the murders that is why he was here. I was going to fight for my freedom just how I fought for my life, God didn't keep me alive to see me suffer in jail and not be here for my son, so I wasn't afraid. He kept staring at me, I looked down because I felt weird like he was judging me, I was feeling like shit, so I know I looked like shit, so I kept my head down and avoided eye contact.

The doctors left and told the family to come back tomorrow because they didn't want too much excitement for me, I was still not in the clear and could easily slip back into a coma. The cop was still standing there and staring, and I had become a little uncomfortable being there alone with him, he must have read my body language because he cleared his throat and started up a conversation.

"I thank God for bringing you back Maurey" he said almost as if he knew me. I looked up at him with confused eyes and smiled at him. I wanted to talk but he kept going. "you know I was at the scene of the crime and we thought you were gone, my partner shot you and I am so sorry. I heard you in that basement fighting for your life and rushed you here on my own because the ambulance was taking too long, I am so grateful that you were able to make it out alive. The other girl isn't looking too good, but she is still fighting too." He had said a mouthful but if I heard him right Nancy is alive, I looked at him and was bugging out because I couldn't believe she was alive, I thought I killed her. A smile crept across my face because God had made me pray for her, I forgave her thinking she was dead... you know I always say God has a funny sense of humor. Had I not thought I killed her I probably would have killed her when I came to for what she did, but I had to have forgiveness in my own heart to get miracle, so I won't take it back.

He told me he had to start his shift he just wanted to make sure I was ok I was so confused because this man had been by my side since he got me to the hospital. I found my voice when he was walking away, "wait Officer! So I'm not under arrest?" I said confused and afraid. He turned around and said "Don't call me officer... it's David, and no you're not under arrest, I couldn't leave your side because I wanted to make sure that you were ok. You are a beautiful woman Maurey... everyone who came in here was scared to lose you. I don't know what it is, but I feel so connected to you, and I feel a need to just protect you. If you don't mind, I am going to come by on my break to check on you, is that ok with you beautiful?"

A smile was an understatement, I'm sure I looked a hot mess, but I was cheesing from ear to ear, I shook my head yes to let him know it was ok to come back. He handed me his card and

told me to call him if I needed anything.

After he left, I started thinking about Cory and Trav and what they were saying to me in the coma, they both felt so bad for how they left me and wanted us to be together when I woke up. I love Cory and I love Trav but what Don had taught me with all his crazy bullshit he caused was that when you love someone you will never leave them, you will never let them leave you, and you will do anything to be in their life. Cory loves the idea of me, Trav loves me but he isn't in love with me, and Don realized he was in love with me too late.

I appreciate all of them for what they helped me learn as a woman, but I will not move backwards anymore. I don't know what the future holds but I will take this experience and live life to the fullest. They all have plans for me, but I have to do things my way, not much has changed its still Maurey's way.

Ain't Too Proud to Beg

Trav

It's been a few weeks since Maurey almost died and it's like she didn't miss a beat. I tried to get her to stay with me, but she took our son and thanked me for holding him down and left the same day they let her out. Money has been happier than ever, it's always important to both of us that our son is happy and that's all I can ask for. I have been meaning to talk to Maurey about how I have been feeling and I think today is the day because I can't go another day with this on my chest. I'm sitting here at this little spot that we used to always go to when we were younger waiting for Maurey to come, we had been friends for over a decade, so I don't know why I was feeling nervous, but I already came this far so I swallowed my pride and was ready to beg.

 I saw her before she saw me, she was walking in looking beautiful, all of her scars had been healing up so nicely and she had a great energy to her. She noticed me and smiled as she walked my way. Maurey sat down and then she looked me dead in my eyes and she had a glow I had never seen before. I was about to confess my love, I swear I was going to say any and everything to get her back but before I started, she said. "Trav, guess what, I think I am in love." I mean my eyes must have said it all because I didn't expect that, I am still cool with Cory, so I know he isn't back in her good graces, and Don is locked up still pending the case. She must have saw my face and kept talking... "I know, I know it's so soon and maybe it seems like it is too soon, but this is different Trav. You know you are my best friend, like I know we have Money together but to me you are just as close to me as my own brother. I love you so much and I wanted you to be the first to know. I am getting married, after my coma I realized life is too short and I spent most of my relationships settling and being with people I loved more than they loved me. Nobody realized they loved me until they loss me, no offense." I shook my head to let her know I understood, but deep down I was numb and at the same time I was happy for my friend.

She has been through hell and I had even been a reason for some of it, my wife damn near killed her and I couldn't help but blame myself. I had to officially let Maurey go, she said this was different than ever before and even though half of me was jealous the other half knew it was true. I smiled finally at my best friend to let her know I approved, she told me how she had been with the cop ever since he saved her life, he hasn't left her side and I was grateful for him so I couldn't even hate.

Maurey finished telling me about her news then asked me what I had to talk about. I decided to cop out and just apologize for Nancy's part in her kidnaping and let her know how bad I felt. Typical Maurey she looked me dead in my eyes and told me she had one favor to ask me, it was to forgive Nancy, I was so annoyed with her for saying that. Yea after talking to Maurey I agreed that I had a lot to do with why Nancy hated Maurey, but I wasn't to really blame for her crazy ways, and I would never bring her around my family again. This was one-time Maurey wasn't going to get her way and there was nothing anyone could tell me to change my mind, yes, I will forgive her, but I never forget. Me and my baby mama had a good lunch at our favorite spot until it was time to go pick up our son. She hugged me, kissed my cheek and as she always did before she left told me she loved me. Maurey is happy and I will live with my missed opportunity with having her ass my wife forever but as long as she is in my life as my friend, I am good.

Maurey

Now that I was done talking to Trav over lunch, I swung by Cory's to tell him the truth. He deserved to know I had moved on. Oh I forgot to tell you guys me and my boo have been inseparable, and it has been like cloud 9 and I don't want to come down. He told me he felt like it was love at first sight and I felt the same way. I knocked on Cory's door and he was there looking sad, like he was. "What happened Cory, is everything ok?" I asked him and he mumbled to me that his father died. His dad was not close to him at all, but I knew deep down that he loved him and needed love from him. Cory told me that after the wedding was called off that his dad had started rebuilding a relationship with him and they were healing in their own way. I guess he must have known he was dying and wanted to get his son's forgiveness, which says a lot about him as a man no matter how many mistakes he made. I stayed a while to console Cory and let him know I had to go, and he started begging me to stay. I had to really face the fact that I was going to have to let another man down and let him free.

"Cory, I love you, but I'm no longer in love with you. You did to me and my son what your father did to you and your mother. You hated him for it and while I don't hate you, I did resent you for that for a while. I forgive you now Cory and I want us to be friends forever, but I can't pretend that I will be able to go back like nothing ever happened. I thought I could forgive you but after a month of suffering I had to pick myself off of the floor and heal my heart and then help heal my son's heart who you abandoned because you were mad at me."

"I'm sorry Maurey, I really fucked up and I never meant to hurt you or Money. I understand that you don't want to be with me but at least allow me to be in your life as a friend because I will always love you and Money, no matter what" Cory pleaded and I agreed to that because my son looked at Cory as a really good friend and had forgiven him. I hugged Cory and let him know I would be there for him no matter what especially with his father's arrangements. He smiled a faint smile and thanked me. That was it, just like that Cory and I were officially done. I had already mourned our relationship so to be honest I was ok, I would always be his friend no matter what. Now its time for my next visits.

Grave and Jail Visits

I got to the grave site and had my flowers for everyone I was here to see. First stop was my dad, I had finally faced my fears and came to visit his grave after all of these years. It felt good to cry and let it all out. I got a chance to talk to him and tell him I loved him. The craziest thing happened, a white bird flew and landed right next to me, and just stood next to me and I felt a presence like I all of a sudden had felt free of the pain I was holding in from losing my father. It was like God had sent me this presence of my father in the bird. I felt like somebody had hugged me and I felt all better. It sounds crazy and I can't make it make sense to you all because it still doesn't make sense to me. The next stop was Nancy, she died last week, I wanted so bad to tell Trav, but I didn't think he could handle this right now after almost losing me and feeling like it was her fault. Well technically it was her fault, but he was honestly hating Nancy. She Killed herself when she came out of the coma, she realized she was going to jail, would never have Trav and that she didn't have any family or friends by her side. I honestly in my heart had forgiven Nancy, on my death bed, so right now I wasn't mourning the Nancy that tried to drug me and get rid of me, I was mourning Nancy the friend, and wife of my best friend. She was never really with Money on her own, but she loved him, I just think she had to deal with the heart break so many times of not having her own children that she was not too close to him. Nancy had dealt with abuse, neglect and just no love as a child, she grew up being a people pleaser and doing whatever it took to be liked and that was how she got Trav. Trav wanted someone who would understand our friendship and not be jealous, Nancy wanted him so bad she was ready to be my best friend but deep down she felt inferior and it started to bring back all of those feelings she had when she was young. I shed some tears for this woman and I literally was scared half to death when I felt a tap on my shoulder. I jumped and turned around to see Money and Trav dressed in matching suits. They came to pay their final respects to Nancy, and I was so proud of Trav. I looked at him with a confused face because I told the hospital not to call him and I paid for the arrangements. He confirmed that her life insurance paperwork came to him explaining that although she had committed suicide her policy is still good due to the contract, she had with them. She had a million-dollar life insurance policy on herself, he told me.

"Damn, you're rich now baby daddy, let me get a dollar" I said trying to lighten the mood. He looked at me and said "No, our son is rich". Nancy crazy ass had left Money all of her money lol. I can't deal with her, she was still surprising us even from the grave. I couldn't help but smile, my damn child was a millionaire before me. "Thanks Nancy! Rest in peace crazy girl, I love you and I forgive you." Trav said and he shed a few tears for his wife that I know he loved but had hated for the way she started to act out of jealousy. I rubbed his back and Money and I gave him a big hug. This will not be the last visit here, I will come more to sit with my dad and yes even Nancy too.

The next day I went up to the jail to see Don, before I went, I had paid for his lawyer and provided a statement letting them know I do not wish to press charges and that he did not try to harm me. I got to the visiting floor before him, so I just got a good seat and waited. He finally came down and I couldn't front even in jail colors that man still looked good to me. He had a certain aura about him that just could freeze up the room for me and all I saw was him.

Don smiled at me and I got up to give him a hug. We talked about the case and I let him know that he should be home soon. I know he tried to take that bullet for me, I know that he beat the trigger-happy cop nearly to death for me, and I know that he only agreed to the "fake kidnapping" for me. He had been the first man to fight for me by any means. He had caused me a lot of pain, he had me chasing him for years while he ran from my love, but he felt like he wasn't good enough for me. Don felt as if he didn't deserve to be loved, especially not by me. All his flaws and his ways that he hid so I wouldn't see the insecure, sensitive, or even angry side.

To be honest, I had seen through him on the very first day I saw him. He had his wall up and was able to trick everyone else but not me. I loved him and even his flaws, I wanted to help him heal and help him grow but Don had figured out I was the one when I no longer wanted to be the one for him. I did everything in my power to clear his name and I wanted him to know I would never hate him for what he did. I would always love Don but like Cory and Trav, I was not in love with him.

He was happy that he had not lost me as a friend, and he accepted responsibility for everything. He didn't care about doing time because he was a "street nigga" as he would say, he would do his time with his eyes closed. I respected Don and I prayed with him on the visit and said my final goodbyes. In the end I got a lot of closure and was able to make room for new love in my life.

Girl Talk

Kim

Hey y'all its me Kim, oh what a rough couple of months, after Maurey almost died we have all been much closer. Right now the girls are sitting with me in the doctor's office to get my results from the latest test they ran. My boo, yes, I said Boo is no longer my doctor, but he recommended me to the best cancer center, and I have since been taking chemo. They did the surgery to remove the cancer and we are here now for the results to see if it is gone. With all that I have been going through who would have thought I would find love in this tragedy, he is almost perfect, and it doesn't hurt that he is a doctor and loves to spoil me. "Ms. Kim..." the doctor called me, and my girls all followed us to the room. This doctor had her head down and she looked so serious and to be honest this bitch was making me more nervous. I mean dang, I didn't mean to call her a bitch but kill all the dramatics and give me my results. She finally looked up from my folder, stared at me with what I felt was sad eyes and I already knew what she was going to say so the tears started to fall when she started to speak.

"It's GONE!" she said with a big smile on her face. "WHAT? "ARE YOU SURE?", "THANK YOU JESUS!" all the girls yelled out at the same time. I dropped straight to my knees and prayed to GOD thanking him for not allowing me to beat by this ugly disease. The doctor said she had run some other test, but those results came back positive and we were all nervous again. "Ms. Kim, you are pregnant" my doctor said, and I was confused and scared for my baby. She informed us that the chemo will not harm my baby and that I should be very grateful for the blessing of life twice. Jaron and I only had sex once and I have been doing chemo and not really in the mood. I was now nervous and not knowing what to say or do, Jaron and I only have been dating for a month now and he has a daughter who I adore by the way. I just don't know if he is ready for a baby or if I am, things have definitely moved so fast. I only told Jaron the news about my health because I was scared, and he was so happy and relieved. We were all going to go out for dinner to celebrate tonight, we had a lot to be grateful for and I was going to tell Jaron the rest of the news then.

Maurey took us to brunch after the appointment, her crazy self, keeps talking with an accent like an old rich

English woman and telling people she has a millionaire for a son, and it has us in tears. We laughed and laughed the whole day. Things were going good for all of us, no matter what the devil had thrown our way, God prevailed, and we were so blessed to have each other.

During brunch Maurey told us that her and officer David were engaged, and we couldn't believe it. Maurey was always going with the safest option and she never really took chances when it came to love but this time around, she was doing things different. We were surprised but all happy for her and excited to know that she didn't allow the crazy past to scare her from finding love.

Tasha told us that her and Greg made up and are using their extra time to rekindle their marriage after the big fight they had about Cory and Maurey. She let us all know how important it is to keep things spicy in the marriage and that we should never keep secrets from the men we love. It made me think about how I was afraid to tell Jaron about the baby news and decided I would definitely tell him tonight at dinner.

Sam was feeling better, now that she was seeing someone to address the postpartum issues she was having after giving birth. She was even able to get Jason to slow down all of the working and help her out a lot more around the house and with the kids. We have all agreed to rotate Sundays to give her a day to herself. Depression is serious and we never want to take it lightly because we are ashamed to ask for help. I think this situation really helped us all realize we all needed a little counseling and a lot of prayer.

Maurey

Brunch with the ladies was beautiful and we all got to share what was new in our lives. In such a short time life had started to change for the all of us. we got closer and our friendship got stronger. After the girl talk, we went home and got ready for dinner and I was excited to have David around my friends so he can show them why I fell in love in a matter of weeks. Kim also fell in love with Jaron quick too, it was so funny because we were the toughest and yet we were head over heels in love with these men. Who would have thought...? I know I would have never guessed it.

After all of the pleasantries, we all were enjoying dinner and each other's company. Kim clicked her glass of water and decided this was the time to make a toast. I knew that she was scared, she is never scared but this moment right here had her spooked. Kim stood up and started her announcement.

"Everyone, I just want to say how grateful to God I am for this day. The great news I got today about my health has really made me so happy. I know that after all Maurey has gone through she too appreciates life so much more. Tasha and Sam are all on cloud 9 with their wonderful supportive brothers and I just want to thank them both for making my girls happy. David, I know you and Maurey may have just met but things are going exactly how God wanted them to go. The relationship you all are growing is so beautiful and I can't thank you enough for saving my cousin's life. Jaron, I know that I tell you all of the time but let me tell you again, I am so grateful to God for you and Kayla. Having you both in my life has changed me in so may ways, my heart is more open, and I want to share more of me with the people I love because of you. I just want to thank you for inviting me into your life, but I wanted to ask can I bring a plus 1?"

Jaron

I was so happy to see how Kim was blossoming and showing more of herself. She was saying this beautiful speech and I couldn't help but imagine marrying her. I was just watching her talk in awe... then she started to talk about me and my daughter Kayla, how happy she was to have us invite her in our lives and then asked if she could bring a plus 1? I was so confused until I realized what she meant, she rubbed her stomach and I realized she was telling me we were having a baby. I was so happy, I was so excited and at the same time I was afraid. I had lost my wife after she had Kayla and although Kim was in remission and cancer free, I couldn't help but be afraid just a little bit. I smiled at Kim and got up to hug her and she hugged me back but looked me in my eyes to reassure me. She didn't have to say a word and I didn't have to either, she just knew what I was feeling, and she knew at that moment exactly what to do. She whispered in my ear, "I'm not going anywhere" and just like that I was at ease.

Wedding Bells

Jaron

This weekend was crazy, we had all flew out here to Hawaii and were all on a little couple's retreat. What Kim and Maurey didn't know was they were coming as me and David's fiancé, but they were leaving back our wives. David was shitting bricks and it was funny as hell to see it. As for me I was so happy, and I guess you can say I was seasoned because I had been married before. Kim was looking so beautiful, I think the pregnancy had made her look a million times better, but if you ask her, she was fat. I loved the weight on her, she was all belly and booty. I knew today was going to be life changing and she had no idea. I watched her sleep peacefully, in a few hours she will be my wife and she doesn't even know.

David

I am scared to death, I have never been in love before but Maurey made me fall in love from the 1st day I laid eyes on her and now I am afraid. I am not having second thoughts, I am just nervous, I want to live up to her expectations of me. She has had a rough life, from the beginning she has always had to fight and always had to take less than what she deserved, and I just wanted to make her happy this time around. I watched her take a nap, today is Jaron and Kim's surprise wedding and tomorrow is ours. She thinks it's a couple's retreat but I flew Money and Trav out so they can be apart of this day. After the nap we got up and Maurey looked so sad and deep in thought. "What's wrong babe?" I asked, she turned around and smiled such a beautiful smile and said, "nothing babe just missing my dad and grandpa." She got like that sometimes and I had to let it pass and console her the best way I could. This was going to be the moment Maurey got her happy ever after and I didn't care what I had to do but nothing will stop me from

giving her what she always dreamed of
and that is to be a wife.

Maurey

The wedding for Kim last night was so
beautiful and she had no idea, shoot
neither did I. I had to tell David a thing
or two about keeping secrets lol. We
had a blast and she was such a beautiful
bride, I mean you guys should have
seen how shocked she was walking out
in this beautiful gown that Jaron had
gotten made for her just glowing and
the baby had added to her beauty.
David and the guys planned an all-white
party today because Kim would be too
tired to have a reception after the
wedding. We were all dolled up, I mean

I had never felt this pretty. To be honest I felt like my dress was too much, I mean it wasn't my wedding reception. Kim was so cool about it though, I told her if she wanted me to go find something else to wear I could, she refused. David had gotten this dress made by a famous designer Brand called Anzel Paris, it was such a beautiful dress and I was just in awe looking at my reflection.

After we were all done getting our selves together, we head down to the party. The ladies and I were cracking jokes on how Kim was walking, she was blaming the baby, but we all thought Jaron had her walking like that. As we entered the venue, I had this weird feeling, almost the same as when I had gotten kidnapped. I started to feel weird, I was confused because there was no music coming from the party and as we got closer to the entrance, I was feeling more and more nervous like something was going to happen, I couldn't figure it out. We walked through the door and there was when I felt my heart drop.

David was standing at an altar, the fellas were by his side, my friends headed to the front and took their place in the wedding. What made me cry was seeing Money there next to David and Trav among the groomsmen. I was ruining my make up and needed to pull it together. I looked around and saw the faces of all of the people I loved so much. I had been so grateful to God for these people, my son was growing and becoming everything his father and I had dreamed. Trav was still my right-hand man, he will always hold the most special place in my heart because together we had formed a life. My girls were all happy now, glowing and growing. My family had flown in to see this moment, my mother and siblings all by my side and it felt so good. David had out did himself. This was my happy ever after and I knew nothing would ever come between me and the happiness that God had in store for me and all of my loved ones.

Nancy

Look at them, they all look stupid. I faked my death and got surgery to hide my identity, flew here to Hawaii to hide out and look what falls in my lap. They think they will have a happily ever after but not on my watch. I saw Trav dressed in a tux and Maurey was dolled up, so I guess they really thought they was going to use my insurance money and live it up. I had to rebuild my strength, make a bigger and better plan and destroy this bitch Maurey and everything she loves. What did y'all think I really offed myself? Hell no, I paid a doctor friend to use a dead body and pass it off as me. Now I want my insurance money and my son, yes that's right. I want the money and I want little Money, because taking him is the only way I can hurt Trav and Maurey how they hurt me. I left the venue before the wedding started and decided that it was time to come home and shake things up a bit.

Maurey could have her way for now but wait until Nancy gets her way.

To be continued....

Stay tuned!

Spoilers for upcoming projects!

Coming Soon. by Cashkakes Publishing

1. Love Behind the Wall By: Monique P

2. Two Homes are better than One By: Cashmere Davis with the help of Michael Davis and Monique P

3. Making it Through the Light By: Monique Chappelle

STAY TUNED THERE IS MORE IN
STORE!!